123 train

Written and illustrated by Andrew Stephens

Licensed exclusively to Top That Publishing Ltd
Tide Mill Way, Woodbridge, Suffolk, IP12 1AP, UK
www.topthatpublishing.com
Copyright © 2014 Tide Mill Media
0 2 4 6 8 9 7 5 3 1
Printed and bound in China

All aboard the 123 train.
It's time to go on a journey again.
One dog jumps on,
he's ready to ride.
Two elephants squeeze in,
it's a tight fit inside.

Three tigers have tickets,
they look for a seat.

They all look quite hungry.
Is there something to eat?

Four monkeys swing by,
two girls and two boys.

The train is soon full of
their chattering noise.

Five hedgehogs are happy.
They laugh all the time.

They sit up on crates,
all in a line.

Six mice with some cheese
are having a snack.

They sit on the train,
all facing the back.

Seven fluffy rabbits
get on with a leap.

Once the train is moving,
they all fall asleep.

Eight turtles talking,
about what, no one knows.

They get quite a fright
as the train whistle blows.

Nine frogs are hopping.
They croak out, 'good-day'.
The train leaves the station
and starts on its way.

Ten cats are playing.
They love to have fun.

They all sit together,
the journey's begun.